Storylandia

The Wapshott Journal of Fiction

Issue 37

The Wapshott Press

Storylandia, Issue 37, The Wapshott Journal of Fiction, ISSN 1947-5349, ISBN 978-1-942007-36-4 is published at intervals by the Wapshott Press, now a 501(c)(3) nonprofit, PO Box 31513, Los Angeles, California, 90031-0513, telephone 323-201-7147. All correspondence can be sent to The Wapshott Press, PO Box 31513, LA CA 90031-0513. Visit our website at www.WapshottPress.org to learn more. This work is copyright © 2020 by Storylandia. The Wapshott Journal of Fiction, Los Angeles, California. Copyright © 2000-2020 Ronni Kern and is reprinted here with the copyright owner's permission.

Storylandia is always seeking quality original short stories, novelettes, and novellas. Please have a look at our submission guidelines at www.Storylandia.WapshottPress.org or email the editor at editor@wapshottpress.org

Donations happily accepted at www.donate.wapshottpress.org

Cover image by Jonas Never (painting), Karl Fredrickson (photograph).

Storylandia

The Wapshott Journal of Fiction

Founded in 2009

Issue 37, Spring 2021

Edited by Ginger Mayerson

The Key

by
Ronni Kern

The Key

by
Ronni Kern

The Key

1

The shopping cart's wheel was all messed up. It squealed and swiveled and jumped and generally made itself a nuisance. But Min kept pushing the cart up the hill.

The cart was loaded with bottles and cans. They were heaped higher than Min's head. They looked impossibly heavy. But Min kept pushing the cart up the hill.

At one jump, two cans spilled out. Gravity grabbed them and they started to roll happily away from her. Min regarded them reprovingly. They were grown cans and really ought to have known better. They stopped. She picked them up and tucked them back into her shopping cart, then threw all her weight against the peeling yellow handle, and kept pushing the cranky cart up the hill.

Finally, she arrived at a cyclone-wire fence and a double-wide truck-gate yawning open in it. She pushed the cart through and up to a high, battered counter. From the business side of the counter, it looked like the cart had arrived on its own. From the business side, Min was too short to be visible. Well, not exactly short. She was exactly the right size for a young child. Which is exactly what she was.

The counterman eased his cigar from his mouth and peered around the cans and bottles to find her. Smoke came out with his words. He was a voice inside a cloud.

"Where's your Dad today, Min?"

"He couldn't come."

"This is not a safe place for a kid to be alone. I could get busted."

Min just regarded him the same way she did the runaway soda cans. "He's watching me. He just can't climb."

"Tell him to stop smoking."

"He stopped."

"That's a start."

Deftly the man separated out the bottles from the cans, weighed them both and then rang up the amounts on his cash register. Its drawer rattled open. He counted twelve dollars and a little change onto the counter. Min collected it carefully, her lips moving as she double-checked his math.

"Tell him, next time he has to come up here. I can't be doing business with no four-year old."

"I'm five."

"Yeah. Well. Even still."

Min scraped the last nickel into her pocket and regarded him stolidly. "He doesn't have the legs for it."

"Then tell him to go to the QuikStop."

"The QuikStop lady's mean."

"Gimme a break; life's mean. Your father needs to man up."

Min hesitated. She wanted to say something, but then reconsidered. "Okay," she said. "Okay."

She carefully buttoned up her pocket and carefully turned her cart and pushed it away from the counter. Even without a load, the wheel was all messed up.

She and her cart rattled up to a church that had seen better days and wealthier parishioners. But in a decaying neighborhood, its spires still intimated grace.

Without breaking her stride, Min steered her cart up a makeshift wheelchair ramp and through the vast wood doors into the vestibule. She didn't pause at the font but continued down the side aisle to a plaster statue of Mary. There, banks of votive candles flickered near the Virgin's chipped blue hem.

Min put all her change into the box, lit a long wooden splint off one of the already burning candles and, standing on tiptoe, used the splint to light the biggest one. She did this reverently. This was a huge deal to her. But there were no prayers involved. Just the flame, the candle, and the smoke drifting lazily upwards. It dissolved into the deep murk far far above. She watched, head tilted back, until every wisp had vanished. Then she jammed the splint into the box of sand where dozens of others already jutted jauntily, went to the confessional, looked under the door to make sure it was unoccupied, and finally climbed into it and up onto the seat.

"Hi, Father Tim."

"Good morning, Min."

"How did you know it was me?"

"I could hear your cart. And then I heard you buying a candle."

"I bought the biggest one."

"Oh dear. Is your father still sick?"

"No. Not anymore."

"That's good. So you lit the candle in

thanksgiving."

"I thought thanksgiving was, like... turkey."

"Thanksgiving is also gratitude of any kind. In this case, to God for delivering your father from suffering."

"I guess... I lit a candle for that..."

"You don't sound sure."

Min was quiet. "Father Tim, you told me this little house was God's house."

"Well, the whole church is God's house..."

"But whatever I say in this little house goes right to God?"

"That's right."

"No people get involved."

"Well, I'm involved... but only as God's intermediary."

"I don't know what that means."

"It means you talk to God and I tell you his answer."

"You, like... translate."

"That's right."

"What language does God speak?"

"He speaks all languages."

"Then why can't I understand him?"

"Because he speaks very softly. Very very softly. It takes a while to learn to hear."

"But I could learn."

"Yes, you could."

"When I get older?"

"It's not necessarily an age thing. Some grownups never hear him and sometimes children do."

"'Cause I've been trying really hard..." She was trying really hard not to cry but the sob came out anyway.

Father Tim froze when he heard it. "What's the

matter, Min?"

"I don't know what to do."

"About what?"

"My daddy died."

"Oh, Min, I'm so sorry! When did this happen?"

Min counted on her fingers. "Four days ago. On Saturday."

"Who's taking care of you now?"

"Me. I am."

The priest frowned in concern. "And where's your father?"

"In the tub."

"He's been in the tub *four* days..." He tried not to envision it.

"I couldn't get him out! I tried, but he was too heavy! So I took the water out. And I dried him. And I even gave him Dolores. But now he's puffing up and I don't know what to do."

"We have to call the police."

"No! You have to tell God to make him better!"

The priest made his voice as gentle as he could. He had practice. There were so many unacceptable deaths in his parish. "He *is* better now. You know that, Min."

The little girl nodded but her lower lip still quivered. She put both hands on it to try and stop it.

"Why did he get so afraid? I couldn't make him not afraid."

"He was sick. In his head. But now that's all over. Now he's safe with God and he is well again."

"Then why won't he come back to me, if he's well?"

This was tricky and the old priest didn't quite know how to play it.

"Because he's finally where his soul needs to be. It's only his body he's left behind him and the police need to bury it. And then we need to find you a home."

"I have a home."

"You're a child. You need someone to care for you."

"No, I don't! I just need someone to take care of my daddy!"

The old priest chose not to push it. "Okay. Where do you live?"

"On 8th Street. Upstairs. In the place with no windows."

"A lot of places have no windows. Can you take me there?"

"Can you leave your little house?!"

"Of course I can."

"I thought... I thought you had to stay in here."

"No."

"I thought you were just a head."

"Like the Wizard of Oz?"

She nodded. He could barely make out the movement through the louvers.

"No, I'm a regular person."

"But no people can be involved!"

"I understand."

"This is just between me and God? Even if you're out here?"

"Yes."

"Okay."

She slid down from her seat. Father Tim punched a number into his cellphone.

"Father Juan, could you spell me? Thank you. Yes, we have a crisis." Then he stepped out of the confessional. Min needed a miracle and the sight of his shoes seemed miraculous. "Okay then, let's go see to your Dad."

The building on Eighth Street had been emptied and condemned and forgotten. With its gutted neighbors, it was waiting for the economy to turn. The higher windows were empty eyes; the lower ones were boarded up with warping plywood. The black ghosts of old arson fires climbed the terra cotta walls.

Min moved a loose bit of plywood cleverly hinged for easy access, and clambered through to what had once been a fairly nice entryway. An Art Deco fanlight still cast a rainbow upon the dust. The vestibule stank like a latrine, but was strangely clear of condoms and syringes. And when Father Tim followed Min up sloping stairs to a second-floor apartment, he found a broom in the corner, and yellow flowers on the table. And a dead man in the bathtub with a big doll at his side.

"Why does he have a doll?"

"That's Dolores. I didn't want him to be lonely. Father Tim, would you like a cup of tea?"

"You can make tea here?"

"Sure. There's water and electric, my daddy was very handy. That's what he told me: 'very handy'. When I was little I thought it meant he had hands all over the place."

"A cup of tea would be fine."

Min went into the kitchen and Father Tim took a step further into the bathroom. The old enameled clawfoot was perfectly clean. There was a can of Ajax on the rim and a purple sponge in the soap dish. But there were spatters of blood on the wall too high for the child to reach. He hesitated, then picked up the sponge. Underneath it was the razor blade. The old priest sighed. Then he slipped out his cellphone and dialed 911.

"Yes, this is an emergency." He pitched his voice just above a whisper. "This is Father Tim from Saint Jude's on Broadway. There's a dead man here... No, not at the church. At 733 Eighth Street... No hurry. He's been here for quite a while... They call him Gus in the streets but I'm not sure that's his real name... Not one of my parishioners, no. He came for meals every couple of weeks... Fine... And you had better send Family Services; there's a child here... Yes, his daughter. Six or seven, something like that... Thank you... Oh. No sirens, please. You'll scare her."

The furious hiss came at his back. "I. Don't. Scare."

He closed his phone and turned to Min. She was holding his tea in a wobbling china teacup. "I'm sorry. I didn't mean it like that..."

"You promised no people!"

"Min, you're too young to be out in the world with no protection."

"You told me, you said 'God is my sword and my shield!'"

"That is a metaphor."

"I don't understand what that means."

"It means He will give you the strength to face what you must now."

She thought about that. She finally nodded. "Okay."

"That's a good girl. I'm going to go down and show the policemen which apartment to come to. Why don't you collect whatever you want to take?"

He left. Min turned to the nest of blankets she had made beside the clawfoot. There was a tattered snapshot thumb-tacked to the cratered wall. It showed a young man and a young woman cradling a wrinkly newborn. It was a window to a past she couldn't recall. She took the photo and then she bent over her father with a terrible sorrow. "Good bye, Daddy. Good bye. I love you. I love you." She kissed him, her lips pressed against the familiar cheek, the familiar forehead. He had been her entire world.

But she could hear the police cars coming, their wheels making popping sounds on the broken bottles outside. Reluctantly, she pulled Dolores from the tub. The doll was huge; she was almost the size of a two-year old. Clutching her, Min climbed through a window and down the fire escape onto the top of a cannibalized Frigidaire. There was a quick whoop-whoop as someone forgot and then remembered about the siren. Min slid down the side of the refrigerator and ran.

2

The sun was slipping, miles and miles away, into the Pacific, but its last garish rays streaked across the entire Los Angeles basin and bounced off the high-rise windows deep downtown. Moe walked through the orange light in a ridiculously orange jump suit. The catalogues would have called it "high-visibility," but the end-of-work crowd, running for busses or texting or lighting cigarettes, never saw her. Somehow, she kept a perimeter of space always around her. Something in her said, "Don't touch me; don't even look".

She turned into a coffee shop. It was barely a hole in the wall, but had ambitions. She handed her thermos to the counterman without a word. His name was Ray. He took the thermos and filled it with coffee, screwing the lid back down tightly. Then set it before her along with three packets of sugar and two creamers. She stared at them.

"So. Did I get it right?"

Moe scraped them into her pocket and turned to go.

"You want a doughnut?"

"No."

Her voice was just as flat and affectless as her face was, but Ray was more than cheerful enough for them both. "I just made 'em. And if I do say so myself, they're delicious. Plus no charge."

"Why?"

"You're a regular. I went to this seminar that said you build your business by building relationships with your customers."

Moe just looked at him. "Don't make me go get my coffee someplace else."

Ray could take a hint. Reluctantly, he eased off the counter. "Okay..."

Moe headed out of the coffee shop and down the street. Her cloak of invisibility was once again wrapped around her. But it made the world invisible to her as well. She didn't see Min sitting on a stoop. The child was staring hard at every single woman who walked by her, then comparing each to the snapshot clutched in her hand. There were so many women: secretaries, brokers, lawyers, waitresses, salesclerks... There was no way she was going to see all of them. And then one of the day's last beams ricocheted off a passing bus and turned Moe golden. It was just for a moment before the thickening twilight became total darkness; but it was enough for Min to swing her picture over for comparison. A ripple of something like joy passed across her small face. Then she picked up Dolores and trotted in Moe's wake.

And almost immediately lost her. Too short to see over the crush of people exiting the high-rise, she didn't realize Moe had headed down the alley just before it. And the banks of revolving doors and clacking high-heeled shoes and gleaming attaché cases were daunting. Finally, however, Min made it through a side door and stumbled into the extravagant lobby. But Moe, of course, was nowhere to be seen.

Because Moe was yanking open a rear service door, showing her ID to the guard and trudging down the grimy service stairs. At the bottom, other women in identical jump suits were collecting their rolling trash cans and mops and sprays. Even the mop handles and trash cans and garbage bags were orange. It was really too much orange for one little space.

There was also a man in brown. Well, his jacket was brown. His tie was green. His pants were the color a man picked out when he lived alone without illusion. Gray and blue and black and maybe some orange too. His name was Walter. Without a word, he held out a clear plastic cup. Moe took it and pushed into the women's restroom. He held the door open behind her. "Give me the thermos."

She did, then entered a door-less stall. Walter glanced over his shoulder at a heavy-set black woman stomping down the service stairs as though she were aggrieved with them. "Yo, Shirelle," he said. "In here."

Shirelle snatched her cup with a lot more attitude than Moe had and nodded at the latex gloves he was yanking from his pocket, "Purple today. Real nice." She entered the other stall. Walter averted his eyes. Shirelle smirked. "Aren't you supposed to be watching us?"

"I trust you."

"That's why you took her thermos."

"I'm holding it. No place to put it down in there."

But Moe was already backing out of her stall. She handed her capped cup to Walter and reached for her thermos. He shook his head. "Wash your hands first."

Moe dutifully soaped and washed her hands as Walter peeled the label off her test results. "Hey, Shirelle, what's going on in there?"

"You ever pee in a teensy tiny cup wearing a jumpsuit?!"

"Can't say I have. No."

"Well, you're a lucky bastard. I hope you know that." She came out with her cup, shoved it at him, and started to leave.

"Wash your hands. And luck has nothing to do with it."

"Man, I'm going out there to clean up *fifty-seven* filthy toilets. Don't you worry your little self about me."

She swept out. Moe deliberately dried her hands on a paper towel and took her thermos from Walter. She left the restroom without a word. The rest of the staff had already headed upstairs, so she joined Shirelle at the supply closet and silently collected her equipment. Shirelle eyed her contemptuously. "We got the same PO and you don't even say a word!?"

Moe focused on wrestling a tangled-up vacuum hose from the closet. "We're not supposed to associate with ex-cons."

"Anyone doin' this kind of work for this pay, you gotta bet is illegal of some kind. The owner's got some sweet deal goin' on."

"It's work." Moe's voice was entirely empty. Her

employer, her employment meant not a thing to her.

"And anything goes wrong, we're gonna take the fall, you know that, right?!" Shirelle headed for the service elevator and punched the button. Moe kicked at a recalcitrant wheel on her trash can. Of course, the last one remaining was the worst one, and followed in Shirelle's wake.

Walter stepped out of the restroom. "Yo, Moe."

Shirelle glanced at Moe. "Looks like you flunked your pee test." The elevator arrived. Shirelle rolled her stuff inside and was gone. Moe took a breath.

Walter watched her approach, her shoulders already tensed for a blow. "That your new best friend?"

"I didn't even know her name until you said it."

"You've been working with her for going on seven weeks."

Moe just looked past him. "You might have noticed I'm not real chatty."

"Give me the thermos." She did.

He opened it, poured a little coffee into the lid, and tasted it. "Pretty good coffee."

"Shop on the corner."

"Be a lot cheaper to make it yourself."

"I don't have a stove." This was a statement, neither an excuse nor an apology.

Walter screwed the lid back on the thermos. "They say you're doing a good job here. Keep your head down. Do your work fast."

"You giving me a medal?"

"Employment's the first step. Socialization's next. I'd like to see you become a human being again."

"What makes you think I ever was?"

"I've read your file."

"Should I be giving *you* a medal?"

"Just keep your nose clean."

"Cocaine was never my poison." She looked indifferent as she held out her hand for her thermos.

Walter returned it unhappily. "And try to give a damn about something now and then."

"I got to go to work."

"Not yet. We're talking."

"You're going to get me fired."

"Not hardly. You're getting a promotion. I'm not sure I'm crazy about it. They want to give you your own floor."

"You think I'll steal stuff?"

He shook his head. "Stealing wasn't your poison either."

"So?"

He watched her carefully. "There's a day care center up there."

She kept her voice flat. "No kids at night."

"But all their things. Their little toys. Their little clothes. How's that going to make you feel, Moe?"

She continued to stare past him but she couldn't help her face changing slightly. "Bad. But I feel bad most of the time anyway."

"It starts to feel worse, you let me know right away." He held out a ring of keys and didn't release it immediately. He was waiting for her answer.

"Okay," she said. He let her go.

She rolled her stuff to the elevator door, which opened just like magic. But she froze before it, unable to take a step.

"What!?" In a moment, Walter had arrived behind her. But it took him another moment to see what she saw: a narrow empty box, a screened slit high in one wall, a merciless fluorescent light humming and flickering. "You did time in solitary?"

She just nodded. Maybe her voice wasn't working.

"You want me to go up with you?"

She looked at him. She knew on some level this man did care about her. But she wasn't about to let that make a bit of difference. "No," she said. "I'll be okay."

And in fact, she was. The long corridor gleaming beneath her mop was soothing in its unbroken vastness. The ring of numbered keys jingled musically, giving her an authority she'd never had before. She unlocked the first office, stepped in. There was money carelessly scattered on a countertop. She didn't touch it. There was candy in a bowl. She didn't give it a glance. There were family pictures. She dusted them, replaced them, but refused to dwell on these visions of domestic happiness. She emptied wastebaskets, sponged the kitchenette sink, polished the windows, vacuumed the industrial carpet. And when the office was as clean as she could make it, she rolled her tools out, turned her key in the door—there was that awful hollow clunk but now she was *outside*—and moved on to the next numbered door.

Midnight was 'lunch time'. The women—and they were all women—gathered on the loading dock. Most of them shared food. Most of them—inevitably— spoke Spanish or one of its dialects. Moe sat alone and drank her coffee. Shirelle sat down beside her and began to power through a greasy paper bucket of deeply fried chicken.

"Barney Fife said it's okay for me to talk to you while we're here." She finished a drumstick, sucked on the bone. "You don't have to answer." She started on a breast, glanced at Moe's lap empty of everything but her thermos. "Don't you ever eat?"

"I thought I didn't have to answer."

"You don't... But you don't *eat*. I've never even seen you take a *crouton*. You don't get hungry?"

"No."

"I would starve. This is physical work and we're big-boned women." She ripped off the wing, nibbled the good parts. "You eat when you get home?"

"No."

"You waiting for them to come around with your Spam? You're *out* now, girl. You can live a little."

Moe finished her coffee and slowly closed her thermos. "I don't feel out. Do you?"

It was 1 a.m., the worst part of this particular work shift. Quitting time still seemed hours away. Moe's body had given up trying to make any sense of what the clocks said. It just desperately wanted to go to sleep. But she stood in the deep dark and welcomed the weariness that lapped around her. It gave even her pain a fuzzy edge. She was totally alone and there were no bars or razor wire-topped walls to confine her. She could stay here forever. Except she couldn't. She clicked on the lights. A huge childcare center spread before her. Photos of happy babies smiled at her from the walls. She grabbed the porta-crib in the corner, her knuckles going white as she clutched it tightly. Then she pushed it away from the outlet, plugged in her vacuum and began to clean.

The first-floor lobby never went dark. Even near three a.m. the marble floors shone brightly beneath the long eco-friendly fixtures. From the street, the floor to ceiling windows gave the impression of an aquarium. The jumpsuits—almost exactly the same color as carnival goldfish—moved back and forth hypnotically as the crew methodically cleaned. And then the lobby clock clicked to three. It was as though someone had sprinkled those colored food flakes on the ceiling. The crew looked up, gathered its gear, and hustled out.

No one saw Min standing on the sidewalk, nose to the glass, clutching Dolores. The lobby was empty and she didn't know what to do. And then suddenly people were emerging from the alley, most of them chattering wearily in Spanish. Min rushed to the head of the alley as the crew branched off to bus stops or rides or the long trudge home to some cramped walk-up. Near the end of the pack was Moe. She walked up to the pedestrian crossing and pushed the light for the signal. At this hour there was virtually no traffic and most of her colleagues were laughing and jaywalking; but Moe waited stiffly, obediently, on the curb.

Min edged up beside her. Now that she could inspect the woman's face closely, she suddenly wasn't certain this was her quarry. She took out her photograph and compared it covertly. The woman in the snapshot was young and happy, her hair a curly nimbus. Moe was a burned-out thirty-something with lank hair pulled behind her ears.

Finally the walk sign appeared and Moe stepped into the street and, all of a sudden, the big ring of keys on her belt loop caught a headlight. Min's head came up sharply. For some reason, this clinched the deal. She hurried after Moe, trailing her a few hundred feet to a city bus stop. Down the street, the bus was hoving into view. Min dithered uncharacteristically. She truly dreaded making the next move. Finally, she plucked at Moe's sleeve. Moe glanced down distractedly, thinking she'd caught herself on something... and saw the sad little girl.

"Mommy?"

Moe recoiled violently. Min's touch could have been a taser. "Get out!" she yelled harshly. "Get out of here!" Then she broke out of the bus queue and plunged into traffic. A horn blared as she ran across the street and was lost to view on the far side. Min, desolate, watched her go.

3

It was just before dawn. The night—dark and heavy as the asphalt it lay on—was finally beginning to thin into morning. Ray raised the rattling metal grate in front of his shop.

Inside, propped against the front door, was a wide-eyed Dolores. Ray poked her with a wary foot. And then realized Dolores wasn't the only one small enough to slip through the grating. Curled up beside her, her tousled head resting in the doll's lap, was a sleeping Min.

Ray shook her. "Hey! Hey!" Slowly Min woke up and, seeing Ray, sat up quickly. "What you doin' in here?!"

Min looked at the doorway and shrugged. "It was safe..."

"No, I mean, what're you doin' on the street?"

"Oh. Waiting for my mommy."

"She *left* you here?!"

"Just for a little while... Later on, I'll go over to her work."

Ray's eyes narrowed. He didn't like the idea some woman had left her baby all alone on these mean streets. He glanced down the block. Only the "gentleman's club" was still lit up. "She work in that club there?"

"No. She works in the big tall building."

Ray, startled, checked out the high-rise. By now the stockbrokers—on East Coast time—were rushing through the revolving doors like salmon swimming upstream. Salmon with shiny shoes and shinier phones.

This didn't make any sense to him so he didn't even bother trying to work it. "Okay. So look, you have your breakfast yet?"

"No." Her voice was small. She didn't like to impose but she was very very hungry.

"I'm gonna make doughnuts. You want to help?"

And it was as though at that very moment, joy had been invented. Min's smile was such a glorious thing.

And then it was late afternoon, Walter plopped down onto a coffee shop stool with a sloping stack of his case files. Some dirty plates vanished nearby, to give him more room. He peered over and found Min, virtually encased in a folded-over apron.

"Coffee?" she chirped. "It's nice and fresh!"

Walter threw a fish-eye at the boss. "Hey, Ray, you never heard of the Child Labor Laws?"

Ray wasn't a good liar; he knew not to look up from cleaning the deep fryer. "Gimme a break. She's my niece. She's just helping out."

"What's a niece?" said Min.

"It means your father is my brother."

Min neatly set a napkin and silverware around Walter's folders. "Father Tim says we're *all* brothers in God's eyes. I told him that made no sense. I'm a girl. I couldn't be anybody's brother. He said it was a metaphor. Metaphor's his very favorite word."

The bell on the door rang cheerfully; and Moe walked in with her thermos, on her regular start-of-shift coffee run. Min turned and spotted her just as Moe spotted her. "Oh, Jesus!" Moe cried. She dropped her thermos and bolted.

Min tried to run after her. "Mommy!" she cried.

Walter grabbed her, but she kept screaming and trying to fight free of him. "That's my mommy!"

Walter's voice was savage. "No, she isn't. She isn't *anybody's* mother!" He threw Min toward Ray. "Ray, get this kid out of here!"

Moe had dropped onto a ledge amidst the overflowing dumpsters in the alley. She was shaking so hard she couldn't light her cigarette. Walter flicked his Bic. She glanced up as she leaned toward the flame. He sat down beside her, put the thermos between them. "You dented it a little but it doesn't seem to leak."

"Why are you so nice to me?" Her voice was faint. All her walls had suddenly crashed around her.

"I'm bucking for PO of the year award."

"Who is she?"

"Ray's niece."

"Who's Ray?"

"Guy who runs the place. Guy you've been buying coffee from for almost two months now... You gotta make an effort to learn people's names."

"What's *your* name?" This would have been a joke if she hadn't looked so gutted.

"You know my name."

"Mr. Walter Meade."

"Mr. Walter Meade the Third."

"There were *two* before you?"

"There were."

"Why?"

"My family was fruitful and multiplied."

"No... why did she think I was her mother?"

Walter shrugged. "Who knows? Kids are nuts."

"I guess I better find another place to buy my coffee."

"The Cuppa Brew down the next block isn't bad. Ray's a little cheaper but hey, you got a promotion, you can afford it... How'd it go last night?"

"Fine."

"Really?"

Moe gazed at the glowing tip as she pulled on her Winston. "Anyone ever hold a lit cigarette to your skin?"

"Is that a rhetorical question?"

"Inside, sometimes they did it to me. The other girls... You know, just to get a reaction. They held me down and burned me. It felt like that."

"If it hurts so bad, maybe I should have them move you."

"I didn't say it hurt. I didn't bother me at all."

And another shift started. What did Moe do when the rest of the world wasn't watching? She emptied vacuum bags, swabbed toilets, squeegeed the inside of windows in the daycare center. Maybe a child-sized handprint stopped her briefly. Maybe she placed her free hand over it; covering, dwarfing, protecting it. Maybe she couldn't help drifting a little in memory. Or maybe there wasn't one. She jerked herself back to the present. She squeegeed the print away.

And another shift ended... not so very different from a mark scratched on a cell wall. Mops clattered into bins. Spray bottles muttered as they slid together on steel shelves. The cleaning crew, mostly too worn to talk, grabbed its coats and purses and headed for the exit. A few of the younger girls jabbered excitedly in Mixtec. One of the older women yelled unhappily into her phone. Moe hung back, the only one in no hurry to leave there. The security guard looked down from the service door impatiently. "¡Andale!" He had other places to be.

Moe took her coat and her thermos and slowly climbed the sad stairs. At the top, the guard pushed her out of the way. "¡Mueve tu culo!" He locked up, cursing, and hustled down the alley.

Moe looked past him, but there was no Min. She walked warily down the alley. No Min was waiting on the sidewalk. She glanced down toward Ray's Café, dark and shuttered. No Min. No Min at the bus stop. The bus wheezed up. Moe climbed aboard and sank down into the first unoccupied seat with no one near it. The bus rumbled on. Moe stared out at the empty streets and relaxed just a little. Now glass and space and movement stood between her and the world.

From the last row, half-blocked by a standing man holding a baby, Min sat and watched Moe. Dolores watched her too.

The passengers dwindled. The man with the baby got off. Min scrunched down but Moe never looked back in her direction. Her eyes remain fixed entirely on the dark. Finally she pulled the cord and the bus slowed. She stood and headed back to the exit. Min deliberately dropped Dolores and then bent to the floor to retrieve her, silently whispering an apology to her companion. She let Moe get off, then darted for the door. The driver had already started to close it. He grumbled as he leaned on the lever to re-open it. "Stupid bitch, you forgot your kid."

By the time Min had managed to carry Dolores down the huge steps, Moe had already reached her SRO on the corner. The bus roared away, leaving Min behind.

This street was a horrible place. Broken glass glittered, only a rumor beneath the thin moon because the street lamps were all broken. There was a dead dog, or maybe a sleeping person, lying beneath a trashed car.

Frightened but determined, the little girl hurried toward Moe who was sorting oblivious through her brand-new key ring. Before Min could formulate an approach, Moe found what she was looking for, and went to insert the key into the door. Instead, she lost her grip on the ring. It fell to the ground with a clang. Min rushed forward and grabbed at it just as Moe bent for it. The two collided. Startled, Moe jerked back. "What the hell?!"

She had two shocks: one, that this mysterious child had appeared out of thin air; and two, that the mystery child would not relinquish the ring. Moe tried to pull it free but Min clung to it desperately. "You don't have to love me! No! Really! You don't have to love me, Mommy. I just want the key."

"What key?!" They were both shouting now as they wrestled grimly. There was no way on earth Moe was giving up her proof that she could not be locked in again.

"Daddy said you took the key to our hearts! And now Daddy's dead and I think I'll *die* too if you don't unlock me!"

Moe stopped cold. She hadn't expected this

at all. Suddenly released, Min tumbled hard against an overflowing trash can. She stared at Moe wildly, gasping for breath around her grief

"What's your name?" said Moe.

"You *know* my name." Min was suddenly sobbing. "You picked it! Minnie!"

"No." Moe's voice was firm. "That's not the name I picked."

Min hesitated, choked back her tears. Was she actually having a conversation with her mother? "Maybe Daddy did... No... Yes! Daddy called me Minerva! He said... you said that was silly. To put a goddess name on a little girl." She looked up at Moe hopefully. "Don't you think it's silly?"

Moe's voice went flat again. "I really don't have an opinion."

"What did you call me?"

"You're not my little girl."

There was a hard finality to this but Min refused to surrender. "What did you call your little girl?"

Moe didn't want the memory but it came to her anyway. "Dorothy..."

Min was delighted. "Like the Wizard of Oz! And this is Dolores. Almost the same. This is the doll you gave me."

Moe took the doll from Min and regarded it deliberately. "No. I never gave *you* anything at all."

The "you" was emphatic. Min mouthed the word, beginning to be frightened. "Did you... did you give Dorothy a doll?"

"Yes."

Min's eyes drifted to the building and all hope went out of her. "Is she inside? ...is she waiting for you now?"

"She's dead."

Min was silent. Her small face showed only compassion and understanding. "She's with my Daddy."

Moe shrugged and bowed her head.

"My daddy was a good Daddy and so now he's taking care of Dorothy. Father Tim says you get healed in heaven so they will both be better."

"Was your Daddy sick?"

"My Daddy was... troubled. They put him in the hospital and they did something to him. And when he came back he mostly didn't know me anymore. He didn't laugh. And sometimes, a lot of the time he was crying. The mean QuikStop lady said he'd lost his mind. But I knew he'd lost the key to his heart. Do you want a doughnut?"

"What?"

"Ray gave me two and I like food better when I share it. I haven't had anyone to share with for a very long time."

Moe put a tentative hand out and touched Min's head. "You've been in the hole."

"I don't know what that means."

"It means you're all on your own. In solitary."

"No, I've got Dolores. And maybe..." she allowed herself the smallest bit of hope. "...maybe I have you?"

Moe regarded her for a moment that seemed to last forever, knowing every single reason she should be sending this child away. But looking out at her desperate street, she just couldn't do it. Finally she nodded. "Okay. Okay, just until morning."

And once again, on that burnt-out street, Min's radiant smile was like the birth of joy, an early sunrise. She held up the key ring and Moe slowly took it, unlocked the door, and let them in.

4

Moe jerked awake, the new day slamming her with all its awful emptiness. Then her eyes fell on Min, asleep on her side of the bed. Moe went still, not able to believe this child was not a fantasy. Her hand reached toward Min yearningly, fondled the tangled hair, the small fingers clutching Dolores. Finally, reluctantly, she shook the child.

Min awakened with a smile. "Hi, Moe!"

"Get dressed. It's time to go."

Min looked at the light spilling through the uncovered window. "So early?"

"I could get in trouble... There must be someplace you're supposed to be."

"No. Father Tim said he needed to find me a home and I found one."

"You can't stay here."

Min frowned at Moe's messy apartment, only momentarily deterred. "But you need me. I'm really good at cleaning..."

"No! You're only five years old!"

"How do you know that? How do you know, if you're not my mommy?"

Moe wouldn't answer. She just got up and started pulling on her jumpsuit.

"I've got to get to work. I've got a double shift."

But with her bare arms in the light, the scars on them were suddenly vivid.

"Who burned you?" said Min.

Moe froze. "How do you know they're burns?"

Min shrank back onto the bed, half-hiding behind Dolores. Moe repeated the question. Hard.

"Min, *how* do you know they're burns?"

"When they put Daddy in the hospital..." her voice had gone so small it was less than a whisper, "they put me in this place. They called it a home but it wasn't a home. And these mean boys took Dolores. And they said they would kill her unless I would let them do whatever they wanted."

"And they burned you?"

"Some... some of them did."

"What did the others do?"

Min's eyes swam. "I don't know what it's called."

"But it hurt you."

Min barely nodded, as though moving too much would give it life again. "And if the police find me, they'll send me back. And then... and then the mean boys will *kill* Dolores. Because they said I couldn't tell anyone... and now I told you."

Moe was silent, as she imagined Min had been for so long, keeping these words inside her. She was cold, as she imagined Min had been. Frozen on the inside by the cruelties she didn't even know the name of. "The police won't find you," she promised. "You can stay here while I'm working. You can stay here, Min. Stay inside."

5

It was supposed to be just another day when Moe plonked her thermos onto the shiny Formica of Ray's counter. She wanted it to seem like just another day. But there was a dangerous look to her eyes and Ray wasn't messing. He took the thermos and filled it. Silently put the sugar and creamer packets down beside it. Moe took them all and headed off to work.

Ray resumed loading a fresh batch of doughnuts

onto the wire shelves. He was still doing it when Walter came in, sat on a stool. Ray poured him a coffee, picked out his biggest bran muffin and plated it.

"Was that our cheerful friend just left?"

"Yup."

Walter buttered his muffin. "Looked like she ate some razor blades for breakfast."

"Must have a double shift. Would put anyone in a mood."

"Except you."

"Well, I love my work. I love feeding people doughnuts."

Walter took a bite of muffin, chewed it, and swallowed. "And here I am, raining on your parade."

"I figure you got hemorrhoids." Totally unruffled, Ray wiped down the counter. "Bran muffins are the hemorrhoid sufferer's friend... That's why I make them."

Walter stopped mid-bite, put down the muffin and pushed his plate away.

Ray glanced at it. "Of course, I suppose some people just like them."

"My *wife* likes them. Give me a chocolate raised."

"That's my favorite, too. Sprinkles or no?"

"What the hell. You only live once. Thank God. Give me sprinkles."

Ray removed the muffin, replaced it with a sweet and shiny ring. Its thick fudge frosting invited the mouth. Walter bit in. His eyes closed. Oh God, this was delicious! But... "I thought for sure she'd be switching to the Cuppa Joe."

"My coffee's better. And cheaper."

"You got a niece." He opened his eyes and looked around. "Where is she?"

Ray shrugged. "I dunno. Maybe she had to go back to school... Or something."

"You don't sound too happy about it."

Ray carefully sponged away a few of Walter's spilled sprinkles. "I don't think the kid is being treated real good."

"You want to lodge a complaint?"

"No. Maybe. Not yet."

"Well, if you start keeping her here, let me know so I can warn Moe."

"Who's Moe?"

Walter sighed. "The broad with the thermos. Jesus, I'm gonna have to start issuing nametags."

Ray thought about this and smiled.

"I like that idea."

6

Down in the bowels of the high rise, Moe prepared for her first day-shift in a sea of strangers. This crew had fresh uniforms and more personable for-public-consumption smiles. Some of the women touched up their makeup. The men slicked back their hair with close-to-hand pocket combs. All of them called back and forth cheerfully—in several different languages—as they gathered their equipment. But Moe gathered bathroom cleaning and restocking material all alone.

And then—like a fuchsia whirlwind—Shirelle bustled in late, snatching cloths and bottles fast to make up for lost time. She did a double-take when she saw Moe. "Hey, you doin' a two-shift, too?"

"Yeah."

"You ever do one before?"

Moe shrugged. "No."

Shirelle whistled. "Get your feet up every

break, every single minute. Even with, you'll be on your knees come quitting..."

She was interrupted by the Day Supervisor who nodded curtly at Moe. "Switch off fourth with Shirelle. I forgot Walter said you couldn't be where kids are."

Shirelle stiffened and headed him off as he waddled away. "Talk to me! You got a *pedophile* working with us people?!"

"That's none of your business."

"It *is* my business! I got a little girl!"

"So did she. And when she was inside, something happened to it; it made her *loca*. Anyway, you know what her crime was. She pees in a cup same as you."

It was the end of her double shift; and Moe couldn't get her arms high enough to lift her bulging garbage bags into the dumpster. Shirelle, wheeling her own up, grabbed an end and helped. "Told you so."

"Heard 'legs'. 'Didn't hear 'arms.'"

"You haven't tried walking yet without your little wheely cart to hold on to."

Tossing her own bags into the dumpster, Shirelle grabbed both "wheely carts" and rolled them away. Moe started to follow, then gasped and had to grab onto the side of the dumpster to keep from falling. Shirelle looked back at her. "Oh, you got that thing goes from your rear end right up your neck."

Moe just grunted in agony. Shirelle watched her a moment and then came back, fumbling in the pocket of her jumpsuit. "We're supposed to have a low threshold for pain or something. But I'd like to see anybody handle *this* crap."

She pulled out a tube of pills, popped it open

and held it out to Moe who stared at it.

"I'm not supposed to take pills."

"Girl, tox screen's not gonna wig out over *aspirin*."

But still Moe didn't take them.

"Then I guess you're gonna have to sleep here tonight. No way you're climbing on any bus..." She thumbed the cap back down and started away.

And Moe suddenly remembered there was a reason she had to get back home. "Wait..."

Shirelle turned. Moe held out her hand. Shirelle reopened the aspirin and poured out two. Considered Moe and poured two more. Then she pulled a bottle of water from her pocket. "Drink a lot. You don't want 'em to get stuck."

Moe popped the pills and drank deeply and finally returned the bottle to Shirelle. There was a pause. She hadn't said the word in a long time, but then she did.

"Thanks."

"You're welcome." She shoved one "wheely cart" back to Moe. "It'll take 'em about a half hour to kick in."

Shirelle wheeled her own cart away. Gingerly, Moe pushed her cart toward the service door which Shirelle was now holding open for her. A couple of the other night shift janitors bustled through, pulling on their coats.

Carefully, Moe put away her equipment, took her coat from a locker, got one arm into a sleeve, and then realized there was no way she was going to be able to reach the other one. She stared at it, then looked over at Shirelle who was seated on a bench, changing out of her stodgy work shoes into something with a heel.

Shirelle frowned down at her laces with feigned obliviousness. "I'm just *sitting* here minding my own business..."

Moe hesitated.

"But I think this time I'm gonna make you ask me... I got no energy to be reading people's minds..."

Moe forced out the words faintly: "Would you help me?"

"Yeah, I can do that thing." Shirelle got up and eased Moe's coat sleeve over her shoulder. "It gettin' any better?"

"Yeah."

"You don't let that driver give you any crap. You climb onto that bus just as ever slow as you need to." She straightened the coat on Moe and bent to do the zipper, for all the world like a mother tending to a small child. "So how old was your girl?" She felt Moe tensing beneath her hands but went right on talking. "Mine was three when I went in. Now she's twelve and she doesn't even know me."

For the first time Moe realized she wasn't alone in sorrow. "If she was alive," she murmured, "she'd be five."

7

Moe hobbled down the alley, leaning on the wall beside her. Emerging onto the sidewalk, she started for the crosswalk... and then hesitated. The lights—strangely—were on at Ray's. She wavered a moment, and then approached. The metal grate was down, but she could see Ray inside, painting one wall an astonishing pink.

Turning to dip his brush, he spotted her, squinted, recognized her, and came to open the door.

"Hi, Moe. How do you like the color?" He gazed at it with pleasure. "It's called Cherries Jubilee. I thought it might make people hungry."

Moe barely glanced at the wall. "You have some milk I could buy?"

Ray was so stunned to hear an actual question, he didn't reply immediately. So Moe pressed on reluctantly: "There aren't any stores open right now."

"Oh, sure." He lifted the grate to admit her. "You want whole fat or low?"

Moe thought. Options hadn't occurred to her. "Whole," she hazarded.

Ray went to his fridge and pulled out a quart. And decided to be daring. "How 'bout some doughnuts with that? The cake held up pretty good."

Moe regarded the frosted doughnuts glittering brightly from the display shelves. "You got anything healthier?"

"I got bran muffins. Whole grain with raisins. And my secret ingredient: finely crushed pineapple."

"Two of those."

Ray put the last four muffins in a small bag and added the quart of milk. "That's two bucks for the milk."

"What about the muffins?"

"They're free. I'm glad you're eating healthy."

Moe gave him two dollars. Glanced up at the board which listed the muffins at $1 apiece. And put down four more dollars on the counter. "They're not for me."

But when she got to her street and gazed up at the third-floor floor apartment's window, it was just as dark and lonely as it always was. Suddenly she knew: Minnie wasn't there any more. And was stunned at the feeling of desolation that engulfed her.

The dealer on the corner noticed as well. "Looks like you're hurting, mama. I can fix that. I can fix that in a minute."

She glanced over at him, looked back at her window, and continued stolidly toward the building. But when she unlocked the front door, climbed the stairs to her landing and wearily cranked her key through a series of deadbolts, she stepped into a total transformation. Her messy apartment had been tidied and cleaned.

More worrisome, there were flowers and weird green leaves spilling from a couple of empty beer bottles. And the crummy wood chairs and table were now a shiny familiar shade of pink.

Moe closed the door a little too hard. She was upset, upset way beyond her own understanding. Min popped up from her blanket, bursting with excitement and glee. "Moe! Moe! Do you like it!? Doesn't it look nice!?"

"Min!" Moe's voice was so sharp it startled the both of them. "Didn't I tell... I *told* you not to go out!"

Min's brow furrowed briefly. "But Wang Taitai's garden had too many beans. I had to go out to help her pick them."

"Who's Wang Taitai?"

"The lady who lives next door."

Baffled, Moe pointed at the chairs and table. "You got that paint from Ray!"

"I had to bring him the beans 'cause, you know, he has a stove so he could cook them. He put them in his lunch special." She giggled at the memory. "He called them Greenie Beanies! I brought you some."

"Cops go in that place!"

"Only Walter. And Walter thinks Ray is my

Uncle. And Ray said he is, too. What's in the bag?

Moe held it out to her, nonplussed by this child. "I brought you milk and muffins."

"We can have a party!" Minnie took the bag, touched the table, decided it was dry enough and placed Ray's bag on it. She got the plate of Greenie Beanies and put them down, too. Then she looked back up at Moe. "Don't be worried, Moe. My Daddy worried all the time. That they'd come back and take him away. So he..." She thought about this, looking far older than any five-year old should have to. "...He took himself away. So let's not be worried anymore."

By now she was pleading. Moe regarded her sad little face and felt something crack and go liquid inside her "Okay, Min. We won't be worried anymore."

8

And the next morning, they both stood half-hidden behind a parked UPS van and watched Ray's Coffee Shop. Min looked up at Moe. "Why is Walter always there?"

"He lives in an apartment down the block. And then he gets a lot of us jobs around downtown so he can watch us."

"Ray said he was pretty nice."

Moe considered. "I guess he is."

"Ray said he was a PO. What's that?"

"It means he works with people like me, who used to be in prison."

"You were in prison?" Min's voice was merely curious. There was no judgement at all.

"Yeah."

"Did you do something bad?"

"Yes, I did."

"What did you do?"

"Delivered drugs for this guy."

"Why?"

"I thought I loved him."

"But you didn't?"

"At the time I did... Then he went scot-free and I got ten years.... He got me pregnant. He got me arrested. And he got himself a new girlfriend..." After so much silence, Moe was finally talking, and found she couldn't stop. "I had my baby in prison. Handcuffed to a bed. They took her away and they gave her to my sister. My sister didn't want her very much. But she always did the right thing. Just like I always did the wrong one. I promised her I was going to change. I sent her all the money I made. I sent her the little sweaters I knitted. I was going to be a good mother. I had my baby's pictures all over my wall. And then she died. No reason. She just did. They said it would have happened whether she was with me or my sister. But I didn't believe that. I believed if I was with her, I could have protected her. Instead I was sitting in some cell 300 miles away... I went crazy. I just went wild. I tore that place down. I think I hurt some guards. They added a lot of time to my sentence. I was in solitary for something like two years. People finally learned to let me be. I didn't want their sympathy. I didn't want their tears. I didn't want anything anymore. If you don't have anything, then nothing can be taken away from you. Ever."

She ran out of breath and words and just stood there and let the memories drain away, like dirty water from a sink, leaving her empty. "And then they let me out on parole..."

"And then you met me."

It took Moe a moment to remember someone

was with her. She glanced down at the child and tried to recalibrate her words. "Before that, I went looking for the grave, you know, the stone; but I couldn't find it. So I went to see my sister. Boy, she didn't want to see me at all. She said my baby was gone and that was that. She'd had a boyfriend back then and he'd taken the body for cremation and then he'd sprinkled it. But now I have to wonder, don't I? If that boyfriend was your 'father' and he just kept you for himself."

"My daddy never cre... cremated me."

"No, maybe that was just the story they told me. My sister was sort of crazy. She probably had a crazy boyfriend, too, and when they broke up maybe he just decided to keep you. I know my sister didn't want you. Maybe she didn't want either one of you. Maybe she's the one who took the keys to your heart."

"Can you call her up and get them back? Can you, Moe?" Min's voice was painfully urgent.

But Moe was hurt. "You want the keys more than *me*?"

"I thought..." now Min was confused, "...you didn't want me."

Moe was silent, then shook her head decisively. "That wasn't me, Min. That wasn't me."

Min regarded her and finally reached her arms to her and hugged her.

After a moment, awkwardly, Moe hugged her back. Then released her reluctantly. "Okay, stay out of sight. I gotta talk to Walter."

Looking both ways, she crossed the street and entered the coffee shop. Put her thermos on the counter. Ray took it without a word. Walter picked a sprinkle off his chocolate raised doughnut. "You got a double shift again?"

"No." She hesitated uncomfortably. "Can I have

your permission... to switch to days?"

"Why the sudden change?"

"I did the day shift yesterday..."

"I know."

Moe regarded her feet stonily. "I liked seeing the people."

Walter finally looked up at her. "Moe, tell me something: how did you get caught?"

"What do you mean?"

"You were a mule, right?"

"Yeah." She couldn't help being aware that Ray and everyone else was hearing her whole rap sheet.

"I saw your mug shot. You were a presentable-looking white woman. Why'd they nail you?"

"I don't know."

"Because you're a lousy liar. So I'll ask you again: why do you want to switch to days?"

Moe flinched, then lunged for what happened to be the truth. "I don't like going home late at night. Well, late... early... in the morning..."

"Someone hassling you?"

"There's a guy pushing H on my corner..."

She stood there as though she had been stripped naked in front of the whole bustling coffee shop. But she had told the truth and Walter could hear it. He finished his coffee as he thought, and finally decided. "Okay, they got an open slot, you can take it."

He rose, tossed down some bills, grabbed a toothpick and left.

But Moe couldn't move. Ray capped her thermos. Put it down with creamers and sugars. She didn't take them. Ray rang up the last batch of breakfasters rushing off to work. Finally they were alone. "Well," he said, "Nothing like privacy..."

Her eyes rose to him and she finally took her

thermos and headed for the door. Ray watched her. "Your friend like the muffins?"

Moe stopped. "Yeah."

"Eat all four?"

"I ate one. She likes to share things."

"Yeah, I know a kid like that..."

Moe shot him a startled glance. He gestured at her rear end. "You got my paint on your pants. I'm guessing the chairs weren't dry yet."

Moe looked back at herself. He was right. She was wearing a smear of Cherries Jubilee.

"Where is she?" Ray asked as quiet as if Walter were still there, listening.

"Across the street."

"And you want me to watch my 'niece' while you're doing the day shift..."

"She's my *daughter*."

"If you believed that, you'd have told Walter. Got the blood test. Done it legit."

Moe wavered. Ray might have been right, but still... "I'm a felon with three years parole. While they were doing their tests, they'd put her in a home and I promised her I wouldn't let them."

Ray leaned on the counter towards her, concerned. "Moe, this is way too dangerous for you. He's got you hanging by a real slender thread. He snips that thread, what's gonna happen?"

Moe gazed at the scarred hands she had wrapped around her thermos. "I don't know. But I'm not going to worry anymore."

Across the street, working his toothpick in a bleak parking-garage entrance, Walter watched Moe and Ray, their heads bent close in taut conversation. The unusual sight narrowed his eyes. Finally Moe emerged but didn't make a right turn to the high-rise.

Instead, she waved at an alley just to Walter's left.

Min ran from it to the curb where Moe held up a hand to stop her. Min danced impatiently until the traffic light turned red and the walk sign flashed its white hand. Then Moe gestured to Min and the child ran toward her and hugged her. Hand in hand, the two entered the coffee shop, a portrait of domestic tranquility.

But alone in the shadows, Walter threw down his toothpick, dismayed, betrayed and furious. "Shit! Oh hell! Oh shit!"

9

And stormed into his district office on that same wave of emotion, impervious to the nonstop cacophony of ringing phones, whining printers, and shouting POs. Until one PO shouted directly at him. "Meade! Hey, Meade! They got rid of your desk." The guy was grinning. "No one was sure if you really still worked here!"

Walter pulled up short at the entrance to the next cubicle. Sure enough, his desk was gone. He grunted and backtracked to the grinner's desk, snatched up his phone and punched in some numbers. "This is Meade, 4139. Where the hell's my desk...? Great. Thank you." Hanging up, he pointed at the parolee sitting opposite the grinner. "He drawing some pay?"

"As a matter of fact, yes."

"From where?" Walter was eyeing the pimped-out parolee dubiously.

"Verizon."

"Which office?"

The grinner looked to his client. The client stare coolly at Walter. "Alameda."

Walter just shook his head. "Luther, there isn't any Verizon on Alameda. Which you'd know if you ever got out of that chair." He started out, then remembered why he'd come. "Who are we talking to now in Child Welfare?"

"Rita James. Wait, no. Rita crashed and burned." He checked the collage of post-its on his wall. "Oh, yeah. We're back to Olive."

Walter scowled. "This is my lucky day."

But at least, as he returned to his cubicle, a janitor was already wheeling his desk in on a dolly. Walter watched the man jockey the desk into position. "I'm not even going to ask how it got wet."

"Sprinklers went nuts."

Walter pulled up his chair. "Just over *my* desk?"

"No, over this whole end. But everyone else got their stuff out."

Walter experimentally opened his top drawer. Soggy papers sproinged out of it. "Oh."

"You probably should throw all of that crap out. It gets that black mold you could lose your mind."

Walter pawed through the waterlogged files. They were smeared and unreadable. "*That's* been taken care of." He grabbed an overturned wastebasket to toss them and found his phone underneath.

Lifting it to his lap, he punched in more numbers. "Olive. Walter... Yeah, screw you too, darling... Tell me, anybody over there missing a little girl?"

10

Moe dragged several bulging trash bags from the service door and heaved them into the dumpster. On the loading dock, her co-workers were well into their lunches and cigarettes. Moe approached the

Supervisor who was frowning at his cellphone. "I'm gonna go and get a doughnut."

"Doughnuts make you happy?"

"Yeah."

"Good. You want to stay on my shift, I need to see some smiles."

"Third-floor bathroom was all backed up..."

"Yeah. And now I know I could eat right off the tile work. But what can I tell you? The suits like to feel you're just thrilled to be cleaning up their crap." His phone rang. He pressed it to his ear. "Yeah, this is Silvio. What's the problem?" He looked at Moe and mimed a smile. She nodded a bit grimly and headed down the alley to the street.

Outside the coffee shop, she stopped warily. The joint was jumping, but there was no sign of Walter or any other law type. Two guys stepped out, talking around their toothpicks and she took advantage of the open door to slip inside.

Ray was ringing up a pile of take-out orders while Min was bussing the three small two-tops. Spotting Moe, she lit up with one of her radiant smiles. "Moe! Look! I made nametags!"

Sure enough, she was wearing a hand-drawn piece of paper plate that read MINI. Ray raised his eyebrows from the cash register. His badge read UNCLE. The letters were in at least seven different hues and got more tightly packed the closer they got to the edge.

"And I made one for you!" Min carried the tray of dirty dishes to the bin at the edge of the counter and grabbed yet another badge along with a rag. She handed the badge to Moe as two new customers slid into one of her tables.

Moe looked at her tag. It read: MO. Min wiped down the table while regarding Moe worriedly. "Did I spell it right?"

"It's perfect." Moe pinned it on and took the two coffees Ray was holding out to her. She put them before the new arrivals, then turned back to Ray with some concern. "She's not handling anything hot, is she?"

"Nah, I got her all tied up naming the doughnuts."

Moe checked out the display case. In fact, each of the doughnuts was now wearing a tiny nametag. They were called Bob and Bill and Lulu and Sue. Moe couldn't help smiling. "No Ernestine, I see"

Ray mock-groaned as he whipped up two sandwiches. "Believe me, my head hurts from thinking up short names." He handed the sandwiches to Moe.

She turned and placed them on the table beside the coffees. "Can I get you guys anything else?" The newcomers looked up at Ray who indicated they should switch sandwiches. "Oh. Sorry."

But Ray was already yelling, "Name tags on two!"

Min hurried up with two nametags that read: JACK and GEOFF. She studied the two men, then stuck one on each. The men grinned with delight but Min was all business as she instructed Moe severely. "*Jack* gets the extra celery salt."

"I'll remember that." Moe did rueful and Ray gave her an amused wink as he handed her another sandwich. Moe looked around. Everyone was eating. "Who's this for?"

"For you."

Moe hesitated, took a bite, and then registered what she was eating. "It's delicious!"

"Of course it is."

Min ran up. "And I peeled the eggs! There's all these secrets. You steam 'em and ice 'em and shake 'em and roll 'em, and then the shell comes off all in one piece."

Ray ripped a bill from his pad and handed it over to Min. "Table One... And bring them a couple more napkins." As she bustled off, he murmured to Moe. "She should be in school. She's scary smart."

"Where am I going to find a school?"

"There's one over next to the park. And with all the illegals down here, I don't think they're asking too many questions..."

Moe looked over to where Min was charming two new arrivals as she led them—skipping—to the open table.

"I'm not sure how you functioned without her."

"Oh, I'll miss her. And my customers will really miss her. But she can walk over here after. Make up nametags for the eggs.

11

Father Tim was studying Min's artwork that still brightened the grim little apartment with its smashed-out windows. "I think they showed up a year ago. Maybe more. I don't know... It might have even been two. At first, he brought her over for the parties... Christmas. Easter. We try to give the children a little happiness. But he was clearly ill. Mentally ill."

Walter was inspecting the jerry-rigged electrical and plumbing, all still in working order. "You saying a nut case did all this?"

"No, you're right. At the beginning, he just seemed like one more man fallen on hard times. He even helped me install a burglar alarm at the church."

Walter raised a questioning eyebrow.

"The poor box is what the police called 'a very

soft target.' Or maybe *I* was the soft target. In any case, Gus hooked up some lights and a painfully loud airhorn. And our burglaries magically ceased."

"You ever consider *he* was your burglar?"

"How much time have you spent with Min?"

"Some."

"Then you should recognize she was raised by a very moral and loving person."

"Who killed himself and left her a helpless orphan."

The priest shook his head. "She wasn't helpless by any definition of the word."

"How do you know?"

"She came to me daily. We talked about God. Sometimes she brought me money."

Walter choked. "She brought *you* money...?!"

"She collected bottles and cans. She was very resourceful. She was under the impression I couldn't leave my little house."

He saw Walter's confusion. "The confessional."

"And you took her money and you didn't do anything to help her?

"I tried. Truly. God knows I tried. But everything I did just made things worse... About a year ago, I thought he'd become a danger to the both of them. People told me he'd acquired a gun. I could see he'd barricaded all the doors to their building. I worried about fires. I worried about what she was getting to eat. I worried about how much she was missing the sunshine, she loved the sunshine. So..." His voice slowed regretfully. "I called the police. And they took him away, and committed him. I'm guessing he was given electroshock therapy. And for a while whatever was done to him apparently worked. They released him. He reclaimed Min. Though Min wasn't her real name just like Gus wasn't his but that's another whole story... So they came back here. And he, with good reason, didn't trust anybody." He fell silent for a moment, then sighed heavily. "And then he killed himself... and I betrayed Min again."

Walter didn't bother disagreeing. "She ever talk of a mother?"

"Not really. From something she said once, I got the feeling she'd been abandoned."

"So Gus, or whatever his name was, might not have even been her real father."

"No. But he loved her as well as he could. And I loved her too... I have been praying so hard that someone would find that poor child and give her shelter."

Walter's mouth twisted. "Yeah. Well. Someone did."

12

The coffee shop, serving mostly a breakfast and lunch crew, had no customers as Moe entered at the end of her day shift. She seated herself gingerly on one of the stools. Ray was fooling with a CD player on the counter.

"You can take a table."

"I'm fine."

"Day shift harder?"

She shook her head. "Just different muscles." They both watched Min deeply engrossed in painting happy flowers on the Cherries Jubilee wall. "I take it the eggs are all named."

"Ed, Ellen, Englebert..."

Min interrupted without missing a brush stroke. "Englebert was too long!"

Ray winked at Moe. "His friends call him Bert. Now we're working on mood music..."

Min interrupted again. "Moe, what's a woar house?"

Moe looked to her, confused. "A warehouse?"

"No. Wait." Min sound-spelled the word to herself. "A w-hoar house."

And now Moe looked to Ray. "*What* are you teaching her?!"

Ray looked embarrassed. "She was reading one of my trade magazines to me. It talked about how the appropriate Muzak can improve productivity. And then she said a German whorehouse used Light Industrial."

Min giggled. "It made Ray spit his coffee all down his shirt!"

But Moe was startled. "Wait. She can read?"

Ray nodded. "She can read."

"Min, how old are you?"

"You *know* how old." She held up five paint-smeared fingers. "Five old! And Ray said they'll probably put me in the first-grade tomorrow because I can read just as good as a 6-year old..."

Ray muttered under his breath. "A 6-year old who can read 'whorehouse."

But Min heard and adjusted her pronunciation. "Oh. Whorehouse..."

Moe looked uncertain. "Uh... tomorrow I don't think you should mention that word."

"But what is it?"

Moe struggled for an age-appropriate definition. "It's a place where men used to go and women made them happy."

"Oh," said Min. Her voice was suddenly shaky. "I wish my daddy could have gone...".

There was a silence the color of loss that neither Ray nor Moe could bear to intrude upon. Then Ray pushed a CD into his player and let Dolly

Parton's "I Will Always Love You" fill the room. And as the pedal steel rang out and was joined by Dolly's plaintive warble, Moe raised an eyebrow. "Is this to push the egg salad sandwiches or the doughnuts?"

"This is for me asking Min to dance."

Ray came out from behind the counter and scooped up the child and her dripping paintbrush. And as the closest Gus would ever get to an elegy rose around them, Ray box-stepped Min around the room.

After a few bars, Min leaned her chin on Ray's shoulder and saw Moe watching them sadly. Moe couldn't help it. It was a sad song, after all. Min whispered in Ray's ear. "Ray. Uncle Ray. Ask Moe to dance, too."

Still holding Min, Ray box-stepped up to Moe and bowed formally. "Moe, would you like to take a whirl?"

Moe flushed. It was possible she had never danced in her whole life. "I don't know..."

"Neither do I. And I'm wearing steel-toe shoes so I'll do more damage."

After a moment, Moe rose and awkwardly let Ray and Min take her in their arms. And so they all danced. And Dolly sang. And the coffee shop was full of a hard-won peace.

But across the street, Walter watched the glowing window. Watched the three people moving together before it. And couldn't decide if this was good or bad.

13

It was a bright new morning. Hand in hand, Moe and Min walked past the chain-link fence around the neighborhood elementary school. But the yard was full of big kids jeering and pushing and taunting. Min moved closer to Moe fearfully. And even Moe was a little afraid.

At the gate to the yard, they conferred with a guard. He asked Min something and she held up five fingers, perfectly clean now. He pointed away from the big kids, to the far end of the weed-sprouting, cracked tarmac.

There was a smaller building there. Its big PRIMARY CENTER sign was reminiscent of Min's happy flower mural. The children playing before it were all roughly Min's age.

Min and Moe exchanged a look. Yes! This was more like it! But as they headed for the center's front door, Min studied the children's improvised games with wonder. In her short life, she had never really played.

She was good with grown-ups though. She sat, feet dangling and hands neatly folded, as the center's director unearthed a ballpoint and form from her desktop clutter.

"Your name is... Min?"

"Minerva," said Min promptly. "But everyone calls me Min. Or Minnie."

The director wrote this down. "And your last name?"

"Mouse!"

The Director stopped writing. "Min, I need your *real* name. This is official."

"But Mouse *is* my real name. My daddy told me: Minnie Mouse."

The Director looked to Moe. "Uh, maybe we should use your name. What's that?"

Moe glanced at her more steadily than she felt. "Flagherty."

The Director wrote this down with some relief. "So, Min, while you're with us, you'll take your mother's name. Is that okay with you?"

But at the word "mother," the air had begun to vibrate. Min clutched Moe's hand and began to nod. Then stopped, troubled. "But if I take her name, what will Moe use?"

The Director's voice was good-with-children gentle. "A name is something you can share. You know, it means that you're a family." Min smiled happily and the Director turned the form to Moe. "You just sign there. And I'll need some sort of identification."

Moe held out her work badge. The Director took down the information.

Min craned her neck to study it as well. "Moe, why does "Flaraty" have a "g" and an "h" in it?"

The Director looked up, startled. "She can read?"

Moe tried to head Min off. "She knows her letters..."

But the child jumped in, "I can read...." Moe tensed. "...industrial!"

Moe almost smiled, having dodged the "whorehouse" bullet, but now the Director was frowning. "She might be too advanced for us. We might need to place her across the yard..."

"No!" Min's cry was sharp and anguished.

"It scared her," Moe hastened to explain. "She had some... bad experiences with boys. With 'mean boys.' I think we'd be happier if she could start here."

The Director regarded her and nodded with understanding. "Did you bring a birth certificate for Min?"

"I didn't...."

"It's not a problem... You can just bring it tomorrow."

But it *was* a problem. "I... don't have one," Moe said.

The Director's eyes slid to Min. "Where was she born?"

Moe's voice became fainter. "Valley State Prison

for Women..."

The Director didn't bat an eye. "Oh, that's easy. I can get the documentation from Corrections..."

Moe stiffened. The Director didn't notice because she was filling in the relevant squares on the Enrollment Form. Min saw it though. "She was handcuffed. They told her I was dead."

The Director went still, looked up at Moe. "Did you just regain custody?" Moe could only nod. "Do we have to be... concerned about interference from the father?"

"No."

"My father's dead." Min pronounced the words sadly but emphatically. "He made his blood come out of his arms."

And the Director put down her pen and regarded the little girl with great sympathy. "Min, it seems you've had quite a time of it..."

But Min had headed down a different path. "Flag-erty. Why aren't we *Flag*-erty?"

Moe caressed the small head. "Min... you and me... we're just like 'night'."

And now Min got it. "N-I-G-H-T. But why not 'light'? Light's better."

"You're right. We *were* night. But then it was day."

14

At the Valley State Prison for Women, Walter sat outside a closed door. In front of it, a uniformed clerk tapped away on an ancient computer. His phone buzzed. He glanced up at Walter. "Okay. You can go in."

Walter got up, tossed down the dog-eared copy of American Jails Magazine, and opened the door into the Warden's Office. The warden was at his window, staring out at the yard. "Walter Meade the Third."

"Correct."

The warden turned. "What can I do for you?"

"I'm the PO for a woman who was released from here about ten weeks ago. Maureen Flagherty." He checked a note on his phone. "Inmate ID W-12..."

The warden cut him off brusquely. "Oh, I remember *her*. She put two of my guards on permanent disability. You sending her back to us?"

"I hope not."

"A PO with hope, that's rich. Well, you tell her we got her old spot in SHU all ready and waiting. That should straighten her out pretty quick."

"I'm actually more interested in the child she had while she was incarcerated."

"What about it?" The warden had lost interest.

"She was told the baby was dead."

"That would be the hospital's call."

"No. Hospital records show the baby was alive at birth and given to a relative. A year later, your office told Maureen the child had suddenly succumbed. That's apparently what led to the 'episode' that landed her in Security Housing."

The warden shook his head with some irritation. "So what's your big question?"

"What proof did you have that the child was dead?"

The warden face reddened. "You think we lied?!"

"Not *you*. The baby wasn't in your custody..."

The warden gave him a savage look, then snatched up his phone. "I need an RP file..." He glanced up at Walter. "What was that number?" Walter showed him his phone. "W12749."

He slammed down the receiver. "This could take a while. We got a hiring freeze in Records."

"I'll wait."

15

Almost invisible amidst the lobby plants, Moe set up a sign that read CAUTION WET FLOOR CUIDADO PISO MOJADO, and then began mopping up a vast puddle that had formed beneath an overhead sprinkler head. The Supervisor clambered down his ladder cautiously, balancing a huge wrench. "That should hold it for now." He looked around at the water and sighed. "The Salton Sea. Great. And this place is full of litigators. I'll send someone down with a wet-dry. We got to get this up before lunch."

Moe began trying to stem the water as it flowed steadily toward the main doors. After a while, Shirelle showed up with a wet-dry vacuum. "Where you been, girl? I thought that double shift killed you." Then she plugged in and turned on and the two worked together, buffeted by the motor's noise.

"I switched to days," Moe said into the sudden silence when Shirelle had to flip off the vacuum to empty it.

"Huh. Was it something I said?"

"No." Moe looked around and then whispered. "I found my daughter!"

Shirelle trilled excitedly. "I knew there something different about you!" She dragged Moe with her to the service area behind the elevators. There was a sump drain there, but also a mirror and sink for on-the-fly appearance-touch-ups. Shirelle pushed Moe before the mirror. "Just look at you. You got a glow. Girl, you're smiling!"

And maybe it wasn't a big smile. Maybe on a normal person, it wouldn't have even counted as much of anything. But on Moe the flushed happiness was as startling as a wide grin. "See that? What a big thing a little one can be. Walter must be *real* happy..."

Moe's smile vanished and after a moment, Shirelle got it. "You haven't told him." Moe just clutched the sink and looked down. "Why not? She's yours, isn't she?"

"Yeah."

"So why? She get adopted away?" Moe shook her head. "Then what? Foster care? You didn't *steal* her, did you?"

Moe shook her head again.

"Then what are you *afraid* of? Moe raised her eyes. They were haunted as she stared at Shirelle in the mirror. "Yeah. Yeah. Yeah, girl, I know. *Everything.* You think we'll ever get over that...? No, not while they can drag us right back in."

She stretched out her arms. They touched both walls. She flattened her hands and seemed to hang there for a moment, crucified. "I did a month in SHU. The cell was just this size. I can't believe I didn't go insane. Locked in, lights always on. No way to see out but those guards always looking in at me. By the time they opened that door, I was ready to claw my face off."

Moe's voice was empty. "I did two years in SHU. And I'll kill before I let them take me back there. I'll *kill* before I let them take Min away."

16

Walter was deep into his issue of American Jails when the warden's clerk came in with a thick file leaking paper. He placed it on the warden's desk. The warden pushed some ledgers aside and flipped it open. Studied the top page. Then flipped through dozens and dozens more. Finally came to one and stopped. "Baby's dead."

Walter leaned across the desk tensely. "You're sure?"

"I'm sure.

"Someone saw a body?"

The warden yanked a photocopied photo from the file and threw it down before Walter. He picked it up and blanched; put it down and looked away. His voice had gone thick. "She was told... Sudden Death..."

"Well, it was sudden alright... You're sitting in a cell, you want to hear your sister just backed her SUV over your daughter?" He retrieved the photo and slotted it back into the bulging file. "It was a judgment call. She went ape enough as it was. It was an accident. Happens all the time. But yeah, if she hadn't been locked up, her baby probably wouldn't have been crawling around in that driveway. You can go and tell her. Me, I got dependents."

Walter rose heavily. "Okay. Thank you for your time." He knew he should leave, but his feet seemed to have lost all sensation. The warden watched him and then glanced down at the file. "Meade, I wouldn't get too cozy with this girl. Used to take six men in full armor to hold her down every time we did a strip search. She was what we call here a real slow learner. She fought us hard for more than a year."

"And then she gave up?"

"She did. But what I'm saying is: she decides to come at you, there's no way in hell you're gonna stop her. Not unless you're prepared to put her down. And I mean: put her way *way* down. In the cold ground. I hope you've kept your marksmanship up."

Walter was silent, absorbing this. Then he looked at the warden. "So can you tell me something else?"

"I can try."

"How often were these full-armor strip searches?"

The warden shrugged. "For this one? Almost every day."

17

But on a summer afternoon, the sun high and the rushing wind even higher, there was no thought of humiliation or confinement. Ray and Moe and Min were going to the beach! Carrying bags and blankets and a slightly tattered and very crooked umbrella, Ray led them on an uphill slog through sand as soft as fine brown sugar. "You ever see the ocean, Min?"

"No!" She was jiggling with excitement.

Ray grinned and looked back at Moe. "You?" She just shook her head. "Then close your eyes."

Min did so obediently. "But how do I know where to walk?!"

"Take my hand. I'll lead you." He placed his hand against hers. She grabbed it trustingly. Ray, juggling his bags, held his other hand out to Moe. After a moment, much more hesitantly, she took it. "Eyes closed." This was even harder, but finally she snapped her eyes shut too.

"Okay!" Ray yelled. "One big step. Two big steps... Three steps!"

Side by side, they marched to the top of the slope.

"Now look!"

Min and Moe opened their eyes to the vista he was presenting as if he'd made it: the blue Pacific stretching limitless and wide. Moe gasped as the salty wind half knocked her backwards, as it blew her hair across her face. Locked so long inside, her soul stretched hard for the horizon. It was something at once wondrous and painful.

"I am free," she whispered. "I am free."

And then, with a yell, Ray took off after Min who was racing for the surf line. Moe, alarmed, took off after them both. Min plunged right into the sea and was slammed down by a wave crashing hard on top of her. Ray stumbled and grabbed her and pulled her up into his arms. "Min, what the hell?!"

Moe plucked the bobbing Dolores from amidst the seaweed. Min was whimpering and shaking with fear. "I wanted..." she wailed, then choked. Ray pounded on her back. She spat up some water... "I just wanted to see what he felt like..."

Moe wrapped a towel around the shuddering child. "What *who* felt like?"

And then Min twisted to look back at the massive majestic wildness all we sensible people call the ocean. But she knew its real name. "Father Tim's Boss." And she smiled. "God."

18

Walter walked into Parole, barely acknowledging his cat-calling colleagues.

"Hey, twice in one week! Meade's finally seen the light."

"Nah. He's seen the furlough list more likely."

"What do you think, Meade? We get shut down, we gonna be missed?"

Walter just fell into his chair and pulled his teetering pile of manila folders toward him. Wearily, he started sorting through.

But the voices didn't stop, unseen but still heard above the too-low, too-thin walls of his cubicle.

"When my Mr. Caruso knocks off another bank, oh yeah, people will be crying."

"Laughing more likely. What loser goes to a holdup with a pooch!?"

A very attractive woman appeared in Walter's doorway. Walter didn't lift his head from his folders. But he knew her perfume. He closed his eyes briefly. "Olive," he said, "what a surprise."

"I'm sure it was. If you'd known I was coming, you'd be out the window."

She sat on his cluttered desk, crushing a calendar and some papers. Walter eyed them balefully. "Reception did warn me, but the windows are sealed."

"No, they're not." She leaned over, unlocked the window by his desk and shoved it open. There was now a gap of maybe eighteen inches.

Walter's glance was jaundiced. "That's as good as sealed for those of us who live on chocolate doughnuts."

"You're killing yourself, Walter."

"Yeah, well, I aim to please."

"It makes me hot when you talk like that, but business calls. I found your little girl for you."

Walter went rigid. She reached into the folder under her arm and pulled out some pages labelled Family Abduction Report. She tossed it down on Walter's desk. He scanned the cover. "Different name."

"Gimme a break. How many missing white 5-year-olds you think we have in this pueblo?" She pulled a photograph from her folder and put it down. "Keep in mind the aging technology is rough but you see anything there that looks familiar?"

Slowly Walter picked up the photo and studied it. He was looking at girl called Min and he knew it. And it hurt. He put the photo gently down. And nodded.

"Where is she?"

"You better let me bring her in..."

Olive interrupted coldly. "I asked you where she is."

"I don't know. The shop where she hangs out is closed for the weekend. She'll be back there Monday."

"Address, please."

Walter hesitated. Olive's voice went low but savage. "Your client is a *felon*! I'll have your job."

"Ray's Coffee Shop on 8th." He suddenly felt very tired.

She eased off his desk, smoothed down her skirt. "Monday, then. It will give the mother time to get here. But I'm warning you: if anything happens to that baby..." She dropped the entire folder angrily before him. "Here! For a change, try thinking about the good guys!"

Walter just opened the file and stared at the same photo Min had taken from Gus's apartment: the happy blonde mother wearing good pearls. This was Min's real mother. And he knew from the size of the file she'd been searching a long time. But still... but still...

He turned to the MISSING PERSONS report and for the first time registered Min's real name. It was Dorothy. The brutal irony lanced through him. He slammed the file closed and held it closed. As though somehow that kept the cruelty from escaping. And yet he knew his effort was futile. "Nothing will happen to Min..."

19

Min was patiently building an elaborate castle just above the surf line. The waves licked at it, licked at it, and then rolled away. Nearby, Ray and Moe sat on a blanket and watched her as they ate their sandwiches.

Moe stopped and inspected hers.

Ray glanced over, worried. "You get some sand in there?"

"No. I just..." She took a bite and enjoyed it. "I don't feel like I've ever really tasted a tuna sandwich."

"I make a good tuna, but the secret is... everything tastes better at the beach. You got your salt, you got your wind, you got your water, you got your running around like a maniac..."

Moe was embarrassed. "Have I really been running around like a maniac?"

"Yeah, Moe, you have. And you know something: it makes me feel happy."

They looked at each other a moment and then looked away. Neither knew where this thing was going. Finally, Ray broke the awkwardness by yelling, "Hey Min, you want dessert?!"

It was hard to believe anyone could pass on such an offer but Min was solemnly packing wet sand around a buttress. "I want to finish my castle first..."

"You want help?"

Min thought about this, then nodded. "Okay."

Ray and Moe rose and joined her, adding towers and scallop-shell tiles, and seaweed flags and other superficial frippery. But Min was frowning, deeply absorbed in adding a new wing. "How many babies are you going to have?"

Ray swallowed a tonsil and coughed. Moe just looked at Min. "How many *what* are *who* going to have?"

"You and Ray. I want to make sure we have enough bedrooms..."

Ray finally found his voice. "You know, the tide's coming in. Pretty soon, little one, you're going to lose this."

Min looked at him and then looked at the ocean and finally shook her head decisively. "No. This is where we're going to *live*."

The words were fierce, desperate, and neither Ray nor Moe wanted to crush the dream of one who had had so few of them. Moe spoke gently. "Min, we're much too big. Even you couldn't fit in this teensy courtyard..."

But Min serenely smoothed down the wall before her. "This is where we're going to live in our hearts."

20

The Parole Office was deserted. Somewhere in the distance, there was the low whine of an industrial vacuum cleaner. Walter sat at his desk and read Min/Dorothy's file. He leafed through telegrams and PI reports and baby footprints and photos and hand-scrawled letters; and with each new page he seemed to die a little more. Then the vacuum went silent and after a moment, the banks of overhead lights started shutting down. Walter glanced up at them. "Hey, cut it out! I'm here!" But the darkness kept moving steadily toward him. "Hey! Hey!" he yelled again in protest.

The last bank went out. He was in the dark.

21

The setting sun was doing its best King Midas imitation, its very touch turning the ocean gold. Min ran along the sand dragging a long length of kelp behind her. She stopped suddenly to pick up a sea shell, trotted back to drop her find into one of Ray's pockets, then led her pet kelp... and Dolores... onward. Moe and Ray walked more sedately in her wake.

An errant wave suddenly curled up and Moe had to veer to avoid it, stumbling out of her shoe. Ray caught her wrist. She jerked away automatically, reflexively. Then looked at him. To her surprise, she realized she trusted this man. And he saw it. He held out his arm. After a moment, she placed her hand on it for balance and bent and pulled on her shoe.

22

Walter stood outside Moe's apartment. There was no mistaking it. Min had decorated the door and adjacent walls with ecstatic flowers. He knocked on the door hard. No response. He knocked again. Finally he stepped away. The unhappy manager pulled out a key and unlocked the door for him. Walter stepped inside.

Between Min's influence and Moe's discipline, the small room was of course immaculate. He walked around, taking in the Cherries Jubilee table and chairs. The mattress on the floor with two pillows, indented by two close-together heads.

And then, beside the mattress, the photo Min had taken from her old apartment. He picked it up. Compared it to the one in his folder. They were identical. There was no question who Min was anymore.

23

Dolores was wet. But she was getting drier. She swayed, naked, in the blast from the Santa Ana machine. Then Moe switched doll for dress and punched the hand-dryer button for another round of hot air. Finally, she decided the dress was done.

As she tried to tug the slightly shrunken bodice down over Dolores' enormous head, however, she saw a door in the doll's plastic chest. A tiny door inset with a tinier keyhole. She studied it, touched it uncertainly. Then she spotted a paperclip on the edge of the sink. She was reaching it for it when Min burst it. "Moe! Hurry! Ray started a fire!"

The child was veering between panic and excitement. Yanking the dress down over Dolores, Moe rushed out...

But instead of a conflagration, she found Ray regarding a circle of stones with some logs inside it. A wisp of smoke was the only sign there had ever been a flame. He shook his head, abashed. "Well, I started it and then I unstarted it."

Moe and Min regarded the un-fire. Then Min patted Ray's shoulder reassuringly. "It's okay. Hot dogs don't have to be cooked."

Without a word, Moe handed Dolores to Min and knelt before the stones, shoving Ray's logs to one side, breaking the smaller twigs off them, and scraping handfuls of pine duff beneath. With a single match, she ignited the mound and within moments had a crackling fire.

Min and Ray regarded her with awe and even Moe seemed somewhat stunned at what she'd accomplished.

"How'd you *do* that?" blurted Ray.

"I used to be a Camp Fire Girl... I was going to be a Forest Ranger when I grew up...." She gazed at the pine trees edging down to the ocean. "I dreamed I would live deep in the woods. And I would learn the tracks of all the animals..." Her voice trailed off sadly. She had traveled so far from those dreams.

Then Min crawled into her lap and gave her

a hug. Moe looked down at her. "And I was going to find lost children..."

Min nodded approvingly. "And so your dream came true."

"Yes, it did." She buried her face in Min's hair.

She could have stayed there forever, inhaling its sweet saltiness, but Min wriggled impatiently. "Moe?"

"Mmm?"

"Do Forest Rangers cook hot dogs?"

"Forest Rangers cook delicious hot dogs!"

"Can we cook them now?"

Moe grinned up at Ray. "I think someone's hungry. For a change."

"For a change," Ray agreed, handing over two sticks onto which he had already threaded hot dogs. "Here you go."

Min looked at the two sticks. "What about you?

"Just a minute. Just stay like that a minute..." He rummaged in his truck cab and pulled out an ancient Polaroid camera. He focused it on Moe and Min.

Moe was surprised. "I didn't think they made those anymore!"

"They don't. I found it in the trash." He was peering through the viewfinder. "Still make the film though, for passports.

"And for mug shots," Moe murmured.

Ray looked up at her reprovingly. "Hey, we're making *happy* memories now..."

Moe nodded. Slowly her hard-earned pessimism was dissolving.

"Min," said Ray, put your hot dog down a little. It's blocking all your beauty." Min was more concerned about burning her hot dog than any picture, but she lowered her hot dog an inch.

"More. More... Okay, perfect."

Setting the timer, Ray ran around to join to them. "Okay, smile!" Ray and Min grinned hugely and even Moe managed a small shy smile. There was a click, and then a whine and the photo emerged wetly. And slowly, slowly, there came a record of their happiness in this world.

24

But Walter wasn't happy. He was emptying his Smith & Wesson at a human-shaped piece of cardboard. Still the target kept lurching at him, like a zombie, like a bad dream. Finally, with a sort of sigh, it stopped. Walter removed his goggles and hearing protectors and stared at the firing range target expressionlessly. Its "heart" had been obliterated by a large singed hole. He holstered his gun.

And just as expressionlessly, he placed a fifth of Maker's Mark on a liquor store counter. The store owner swiped it across the scanner, took Walter's credit card and swiped that also, as though none of this meant anything at all. "Two nights in a row?"

"Yeah."

"Was that my last bottle?"

It was an effort to answer. "I guess so."

"Should I be ordering more?"

Walter thought about this. The thinking didn't make him happy. "I don't know."

The store owner nodded, handed Walter's card back and started bagging the whisky. "I'll take that as a 'yes.'"

25

Min and Dolores and Moe and Ray lay side by side in Ray's truck bed. They had blankets for warmth and a million stars for light.

"Ray," asked Min, "can we pick more shells tomorrow?"

"Sure. The tide 'll be out when we get up."

"And then what will we do?"

"We'll jump up and down in the waves until we're all exhausted."

"Maybe," said Moe, "we should let Dolores stay on the beach and watch our towels..."

"Yeah," said Min. "I don't want her to pucker,"

This gave the adults pause. They remembered the last loved one Min had seen "pucker." Ray changed the subject. "And then we'll watch Moe build another amazing fire."

"What will we cook?"

"What's your favorite?"

"Grilled cheese sandwiches!"

"Grilled cheese sandwiches with seaweed?"

"No!" protested Min, "The seaweed has bugs!"

"And then we'll go to the merry-go-round and say goodbye to Silver and Shazam." Ray looked to Moe. "What was your horse's name?"

"Petunia."

"We'll say good-bye to Petunia. And then we'll pick strawberries. On the way home. Enormous red sweet strawberries."

Min liked this idea. "Can we eat some?"

"You can eat as many as you want. The rest we'll bring back and I'll make strawberry shortcake for my customers."

"Can I help?" said Min.

"Unh-unh, you'll be sleeping. You have school on Monday. But maybe before you go, you can whip the cream."

They lay there looking at the stars. Min sighed contentedly. "Ray, this was the best time I ever had."

"Me too, Min."

Moe regarded the two of them. "And me three."

Min snuggled up to her. "I wish we could stay here forever."

"The beach will always be here," Moe assured her.

"And my castle."

"And your castle."

"In our hearts..." Min's voice was getting vague as she started to drop off. "Moe?"

"Yeah?"

"I don't think Petunia is a good name for your horse. Petunia is a *flower*. If you sat on a flower you would squoosh it..."

Ray grinned at Moe over Min's head. "I guess you better pick another name."

"Cassiopeia."

"What's that!?" Min was suddenly awake again.

Moe regarded the heavens. "Queen of the Night. See that W? That's Cassiopeia right there. And see, there's the Dipper. It looks just like Ray's big soup ladle."

"You're just like my Daddy. You know everything!"

"No," said Moe. "I know some things... I know I love you."

Min was starting to drop off again. "But the ladle's upside down. All the soup will fall out."

"No, there's no gravity up there. Nothing falls. Everything stays just where it is... forever."

"No running and jumping?"

"No."

"I don't like that. I think it sounds scary."

And she was asleep. Moe remembered her past.
"It is."

26

Walter sat behind the wheel of his car and emptied the last of his Maker's Mark into the tumbler on his dashboard. Squinted heavy-eyed up toward Moe's still-dark apartment. And then drank.

Somewhere church bells were ringing. He looked out his window to see dressed-up adults and children heading for communion. He was unshaven, rumpled, and sweaty. He hated everything about this planet. He opened his fliphone and dialed.

"How you doin', Bo? It's Walter Meade... Your parole officer... Yeah, *that* Walter Meade. Your boss said you stayed home sick on Friday.... You see a doctor...? You going in tomorrow...? You still feel bad, you better come in and see *me*. No, I'm not a doctor but I can revoke your ass right back to San Q if I think you're jiving me... What can I tell you, Bo? I'm getting mean."

He closed his phone and threw it across the front seat. Then he leaned back and closed his eyes.

It was already dark when Ray struggled to lift the sleeping Min from the cab of his pickup. "Boy, we're lucky they didn't weigh her. I think she ate twice the strawberries we paid for..."

He carried the child around to the back where Moe was extracting towels and plastic bags of seashells from amidst the dozens of flats of fresh-picked strawberries. "Take that top flat there..."

"I have no fridge..."

"I don't think that will be a problem. Look at

her face."

They both did. Min's lips were stained red from all the ripe fruit. And as she snuggled against Ray, she spread the redness onto his t-shirt. Moe tried to wipe it off with one of the towels. "Ray, this was really nice of you."

"It was nice of you to come."

"Why do you bother with us?"

"I like you. I like both of you. Easy as that."

Moe suddenly bent toward him and kissed him. She was as surprised as he. "I didn't think I remembered how to do that!"

"You know you didn't have to..."

"I know. But I like you. Easy as that."

And together, companions... friends... Min's make-shift family... they headed for the tenement. Moe unlocked the front and then led them up the dark stairs.

At the top, however, she could see a sliver of moon falling—illogically—onto the unlit landing. There was no window. And then she realized the door to her apartment was ajar. Apprehensive, she approached it and pushed it open with her fingertips. And flinched. Walter was standing inside. But not a Walter she knew. A cold Walter. An angry Walter. A beaten Walter. "Can you read?"

"Yeah, I can read."

"Then I want you to read something." He hoisted the thick file from the table and held it out to her.

"What is it?"

"It's a story. It goes like this: 'Once upon a time there was a little girl. And she had a mommy and she had a daddy. And her mommy worked for a big corporation...'" Moe stiffened but Walter plowed on.

"And her daddy was an inventor so he stayed home with the little girl and raised her..."

"No!" Moe threw out an arm, trying to block Walter from getting near Min who was in Ray's arms behind her. The strawberries went flying. "No! She's mine! Her daddy was a coked-up thug!"

Walter looked past Moe to Ray who was standing bewildered in the doorway. "Put Min to bed." He grabbed Moe, dragged her into the hallway, and shook her angrily. "And what was *Dorothy's* mother?!"

Moe wept and fought him. "Don't take her! Please don't take her!"

Ray emerged from the apartment. He was ashen. "I thought you were her friend..."

"No. I'm her parole officer. And I'm giving her a chance to do the right thing." He turned on Moe again. "Read the file. It's about a woman... a mother just like you...who lost her daughter because her husband went nuts and took her baby and changed her name so many times that nobody could find her."

Moe was sobbing. "*I* found her..."

"Yeah. And now you're going to give her back."

"No!"

"Yeah, you are, Moe. They'll be coming for her in the morning..." Walter glanced at Ray. "And you, unless you want to be accessory to all kinds of trouble, get out of here."

Ray looked to Moe, wavering. But she was already turning back into something inanimate. "Go. You got your breakfasts to get cooking. Go."

Ray left reluctantly. Walter hesitated, then followed him. But Moe just stood in the narrow hall. After a moment, she put her hands up to brace herself against the walls closing in on her. She was in hell again.

And then it was Monday. Walter sat on a stool at Ray's coffee shop. Ray, silent, put a cup of coffee in front of him. Both of them looked like they hadn't slept in weeks. Ray poured out two to-go coffees for waiting customers, took their money and slotted it into his cash register; then plated one chocolate raised and set it carefully down before Walter.

Walter stared at it balefully. "You poison it?"

"Last one. I don't want you to come here anymore."

Walter picked up his doughnut and nodded his understanding.

Olive came in and sat down beside Walter. "So how's the coffee?"

"Good. I'm going to miss it."

She nodded at Ray who flipped her cup and filled it.

"Ray," said Walter, "this is my ex."

Olive eyed the chocolate raised and then Ray. "You're going to kill him with those doughnuts."

"I hope so."

"You see that, Liv? Another member for your fan club."

"Where's Dorothy?"

"Where's the mother?"

"Flying in from Beijing. Her plane got held up. But she should be here any minute. So.."

Walter bit into his doughnut bitterly. "I'm not giving the kid to *you*."

"Okay," she said. "We'll wait." She sipped her coffee. Broke off a piece of Walter's doughnut and ate it. Looked at him. "You look like hell."

"I feel like hell."

"You drinking again?"

"Only when you give me reason."

"You care about the wrong people."

Walter shook his head. "No. I care about everyone. I even cared about you."

"Where's the child?"

"I told Moe we'd come to the apartment..."

Olive recoiled. "You *told* her?!"

"Yeah."

Olive jumped up, outraged. "And you think she'll still be there?!"

Walter steadily worked his way through his doughnut. "I don't know."

"Damn you! You don't know and you don't care, do you? Did you even read her letters?!"

"I did."

Olive looked past him out the window, saw the cab pulling up. "Here she is. *You* go and talk to her. *You* tell her you've lost her little girl. Again. You tell her she'll be crying for three more years!"

Walter took out his Smith & Wesson and pulled back the slide to check for copper in the chamber. Then he reholstered it. "Do me a favor and just follow me." He got up and left the shop.

Ray looked after him, then took off his apron and turned the sign on the door to CLOSED. He looked at Olive. "I'm leaving. You staying?"

She got up and left. Ray locked the door behind them both.

But on the street, Shirelle was hurrying up, her eyes wide at the sight of Olive's car with its FAMILY SERVICES logo. "Walter..." She tried to stop him. "Walter, you're taking Min!?"

"Shirelle, get out."

"She said she'd kill. Moe said she'd kill before she let you."

"Shut up!"

But Olive had heard and was already pulling out her cellphone. "I'm calling for backup!"

Furious, Walter jumped into his car and screeched away.

Not knowing where to send the cavalry, Olive hurried to the newly-arrived taxi and slid into the backseat. Ray and Shirelle scrambled into Ray's truck.

27

Moe stood at her window and watched all the vehicles arriving. Then she looked back at Min who was frowning in concentration at her sneakers. "Min, it's time to go."

"The nose on my sneaker string broke and it won't go through the holes now."

Moe sat down beside her and bent to lick the tip of Min's lace. Then she twisted it into a point so she could thread it. There were several holes and it took her quite a while. An affectionate child, Min patted Moe's hair while she was doing this. Moe tried not to hear the urgent footsteps in the hall. She tried not to hear the key in the lock and the door starting to open. But when it slammed hard into the wall, both she and Min jumped.

Walter stepped into the room with his gun up. But taking in the tender scene, he lowered it so Min couldn't see it. She lit up. "Hi, Walt! Ray's making strawberry shortcake!"

Walter looked to Moe. He kept his voice low. "She's here."

Moe rose as though every bone in her weighed over a hundred pounds now. "Min, take Dolores."

"Miss Enriquez said Dolores was too young to

come to school..."

Walter said, "It's okay today."

And Min finally registered the terrible tension in both these grown-ups. She went still, obediently picked up Dolores and took Moe's hand.

Walter looked at the tightly clasped hands and something in him died a little further. He gestured to Moe covertly with his gun. "You go first."

Moe gazed briefly at her jumpsuit hanging on a peg, at the ring of keys dangling beside it... She wouldn't need either of them any more. She led Min to the door... down the stairs... and onto the street. Walter remained in the doorway behind them.

Min blinked at the bizarre collection of police cruisers and cars and taxis and strangers strewn all around. Suddenly she spotted Ray. She gazed at him, confused. And then her eye was attracted by a woman launching herself out of the taxi. She had Min's wild hair and cat-green eyes. She was crying. "Dot! Dorothy! Little D!"

Olive tried to restrain her but Min's mother ran straight to her daughter. Min shrank back against Moe. Min's mother fell to her knees in the street. "Dottie! I'm your mommy!"

She tried to reach for her child, but Min shrank back further. "No. Moe is my mommy."

Min's mother glanced up at Moe. Her eyes were red-rimmed and tragic. Moe saw herself in them. Then the woman looked back to Min. "But I have the key! The key to your heart!"

She reached into her blouse and pulled out a small gold key hanging from her neck on a thin chain. The key glinted in the morning sun. Min stared at it, uncertain. The strange woman reached out. She was almost whispering. "Give me Dolores..."

Min handed over her doll without a word. Min's mother pushed up Dolores' dress and inserted the key into the tiny keyhole. It fit perfectly. With a small turn and smaller click, the door opened wide.

Min released a breath she hadn't even known she was holding. She looked up into the woman's face. "Mommy..." The word was the sigh of a lost child coming home. She collapsed into her mother's arms and the woman embraced her. Moe watched, swaying with the effort of doing nothing at all.

Min clutched her mother tightly. "But where *were* you?!"

"China. I was working in China."

Min just nodded. "That's what Dolores said."

"Dolores?"

Min took her doll and turned her over. On her back was clearly stamped: MADE IN CHINA. "I tried to dig to you one time. You were too far. But why... did you go away from us?

"I didn't, baby! I didn't! I've been looking for you every day! It's just Daddy and I..." She broke off. How could she explain what was beyond even her own understanding? "I didn't know he was already getting sick. And he loved you so much and I knew China was going to be so different. I let him keep you just until I got settled in my new job. But by the time I was... he'd taken you. He'd taken you away and I couldn't find you."

"And..." Min asked uncertainly, "are you going back to China now?"

"No. I'm staying here. With you."

She looked up at Moe. "I'm going to stay in LA and I hope you will visit us often."

Moe nodded noncommittally. Min looked to her and suddenly realized she was going to be taken away from Moe and Ray and this whole life she had cobbled together. She froze.

But her mother was already rising. "Dot, say goodbye to your friend..."

Min looked at her mother, bewildered. Moe was not her 'friend'. Moe was her everything. So she looked to Ray who was approaching so she could hug him. Then he gently led her to Moe. Min hugged Moe's knees tight. Moe didn't bend. She was already disappearing into some hard place inside herself. Min felt it and her face scrunched into grief.

Ray knelt at her side. "Don't forget the castle. In our hearts, we'll always live there."

Min nodded. He started to turn her back to her mother. But suddenly, convulsively, Moe reached for the child and hugged her hard. Hugged her as though she were her own child she never got to hold for even a minute. And then she released Min. Min walked to her mother. The two of them got into the taxi. It pulled away.

Moe and Ray could see Min kneeling on the seat, looking back at them. And then the taxi and Min were gone.

Walter came up beside Moe. She didn't look at him but she knew he was there. "Thank you for not arresting me in front of her."

"I'm not arresting you, Moe. I'm recommending you for early discharge." He looked at Olive and Shirelle and the police presence that—unneeded— was dispersing. For the first time, Olive regarded him with something like understanding. He said, "I think we're all gonna be okay."

But in the taxi, Min watched the only world she had ever known speeding away from her. She turned from the back window and sat sadly beside her mother. "We're going to miss Ray's strawberry shortcake now..."

"We'll go back to see them," said her mother.

But Min just nodded. She had learned to doubt grownups and their promises. After a moment, she took Dolores from her mother.

Her mother glanced down at the doll. "I'm going to miss wearing that key. It made me feel like I was always close to you..."

Min pushed up Dolores' dress and turned the key to remove it. She handed it up to her mother.

"Thank you, Dot."

Min leaned against her mother uncertainly. She wasn't sure who this "Dot" was. Then she noticed Dolores' dress was still pushed up. She went to lower it and discovered that, in removing the key, she had actually unlocked the doll's heart. The little door stood open. And inside, Min could see something white.

She reached in and pulled out... a folded photograph. She straightened it out on her knee as her mother leaned past her, to tell the cabbie their destination.

It was the Polaroid picture Ray had taken at the campsite: all three of them smiling together, happy as loons.

She replaced the picture inside the doll and pushed the door shut. It stayed closed without locking. Then she pulled down Dolores' dress and clutched the doll to her side. And finally leaned against this woman whom she couldn't remember. She was an affectionate child and in time would learn to love her. But in Dolores' heart, she and Moe and Ray would always be together. Even when Min forgot—and she would—they would still be there.

An award-winning screenwriter for more years than she cares to remember, Ronni Kern is now an anaphylactic beekeeper and —equally perversely—writes novels and novellas just because. You can read more of her work at www.farmfreshpress.com.

Thank you to the Wapshott Press sponsors, supporters, and Friends of the Wapshott Press.

Muna Deriane
Kit Ramage
Rachel Livingston
Kathleen Warner
Ann and John Brantingham
David Meischen
John O'Kane
Thomas Loper
Laurel Sutton
James Wilson
Alice Frances Wickham
James Wilson
Suzanne Siegel
Toni Rodriguez
James and Rebecca White
Leslie Bohem
Robert Earle and Mary Azoy
Phil Temples
Richard Whittaker
Ann Siemens
John Grigor Bell

The Wapshott Press is a 501(c)(3) not-for-profit press publishing work by emerging and established authors and artists. We publish books that should be published. We are very grateful to the people who believe in our plans and goals, as well as our hopes and dreams. Our website is at www.WapshottPress.org. Donations gratefully accepted at www.Donate.WapshottPress.org.

www.ingramcontent.com/pod-product-compliance
Lightning Source LLC
Chambersburg PA
CBHW051312170626
46809CB00004B/1871